~~~

Halo's Story

~~~

by Bob Wolf

ISBN: 1456503340
ISBN 13: 978-1456503345

Preface

~~~

In the first century, a litter of puppies was born to a common dog. One puppy was chosen and given to a young man of sixteen years; His name was Jesus, the son of a carpenter.

Jesus accepted responsibility for this puppy and their Love for one another began. Throughout seventeen years this dog seldom left Jesus' side; he was there during the years Jesus helped His father, Joseph, work to feed his family.

Halo learned of all the different kinds of Love by watching and listening to his Master. Jesus taught thousands and His ministry grew during many journeys around Galilee and the Middle Eastern area. Halo tells the story of his life with Jesus.

~~~

To Kids Everywhere

CHAPTER ONE

Our Names

~~~

With eyes closed and dozing in and out of consciousness, I felt the warm, loving hands of my new master holding me. In days to come, many hands held me, but none felt so good as Master's – His were different.

The place where I sleep is cozy and warm and best of all it's under Master's bed. At night I can hear Master breathe when He sleeps. I'll never be alone while Master is near.

After a while I learned that Master's name was "Jesus." He was 16 years old and He lived with His family in a place called Nazareth. I guess that's where I live too. I play with many children every day, rolling in the dust and running after their little feet. Mostly I like following Master and watching Him work with His father; they make things for people.

I still don't understand too good, but Master seems to have two fathers; one of them is with Him all the time, but we can't see Him. The other one helps Him build things.

I hope some day Master will show me His other Father. He sounds like a very interesting person.

For many, many days my name was "Puppy." I learned that name and paid attention when I heard that word. Then it seemed my name changed. One day, all at once people called me "Halo." I don't know why. These people I live with are sometimes very odd, but I still prefer them to the other animals like me.

I think Master has another name too. I've heard people call Him "Rabbi." His family still calls Him "Jesus" though. Master also has a very important job. He makes people well when He talks to His other Father. No one else does this. I've heard Master tell people that a thing called Love is the most important thing in the whole world for all people to know about. I'm starting to think this Love thing is the way I feel towards Master and the people in His family. His family must feel love for me too.

Today I heard the Great Lady, Jesus' mother, explaining to her friend how I received my new name of "Halo." She said it was because I chase my tail a lot, whatever that means. I also Like to chase bugs. Me and my animal friends are going bug hunting later this evening, when the bugs come out to play. They're fun to catch and then we let them go. Master said to be gentle with them so they don't get hurt. Master loves everything in this life. Tomorrow Master says we will go on a short journey to another village and visit a person who needs Him desperately. I heard Master use the word "heal" so I guess that's what is going to happen when we get there.

CHAPTER TWO

Healing
~~~

    The journey to this village with Master was fun; He threw rocks and I chased them all the way here.

    This village is much smaller than ours and the people here are very old and they don't feel well at all. Letting these people touch me and pet me makes them feel much better. Master says those things on their faces and hands will go away because Master brought me and His Father to visit; you know, the Father we can't see with our eyes. These people love the Father and Master so much that they are crying; they're serious about this thing called Love. When we got home, I tried telling my animal friend about our journey and what Master did for the people there, but he wouldn't hold still long enough; he had some bugs on the run. I'm glad I taught my animal friend not to hurt the bugs we catch. That way we can catch them again another day and we won't run out of them.

My animal friends tell me I have the best home in all of Nazareth, because I get to sleep inside and have table scraps for dinner every evening. I thought all animals had a family to love them and care for them.

I'm very fortunate to have Master and His family to make my life so pleasurable. Master told me that all animals and people will have a wonderful place to go, after we are done living in Nazareth. It's the place where the other Father lives. Master said I'll see more Love there than I can imagine. I'm looking forward to that new home; I hope there will be bugs to chase and children to play with in the warm morning sun. Master is so smart about everything; I'm going to keep following Him 'cause He knows just what I need.

CHAPTER THREE

Lost

~~~

I followed Master today toward a group of people who had gathered; we stood and listened to a woman speak about her little girl who hadn't been seen since the evening before. The woman was crying and shaking and I could tell she didn't feel well at all. Master pushed forward to the woman and put His arm around her. He said to her that He and Halo would go looking for her daughter. He said that the little girl was as good as found already. Master instructed me to go find my animal friends and meet Him at the well where the water comes from.

After rounding up three of my friends, we all headed toward the well where we found Master and six other men with sticks in their hands. Each of my friends was put in charge of two men.

Me and Master were a team of our own. We all set off in different directions and agreed to meet at the well when the sun touched the top of the big hill.

After many hours of chasing bugs and retrieving rocks thrown by Master, He asked me if my nose detected the little girl. I shook my head from side to side. We turned this way and that looking for any sign of her. The sun wasn't even close to the hill when Master sat down and drank from His bag; I got some too. Master's water was wonderful and helped me want to continue the search.

Suddenly I heard the galloping sound of my big animal friend's floppy feet. He ran directly over the top of me, knocking me down and jumped on top of Master, knocking Him to the ground, licking Him all over His face and head.

Master roared with laughter as He got up dusting Himself off. He hugged my friend and thanked him for the message. "Come on, Halo" Master said, "our work is complete." There was a different and good feeling in the air as the three of us leisurely strolled back home. My big animal friend doesn't understand the pleasure in chasing bugs or retrieving rocks; oh well, different games for different animals.

Upon arriving back at the village, we found mother and daughter reunited and in good health. Master was thanked by the mother and daughter and the crowd of others nearby.

Master once again explained to me that the Father was to thank for the happy ending this day. Maybe Master will teach me to talk to the Father; but, then again perhaps I don't need to, because I don't have problems like people do.

CHAPTER FOUR

Bugs

~~~

    Tomorrow is the day when my family goes to the place called Temple, where they become close to and talk to the Father. It's a special day for most of the people in our village. I want to go inside and see the Father too, but Master says I still won't be able to see Him yet. Master asked me to do a very special job while all the people are inside the building. He said I should keep all the bugs from coming inside while everyone visits the Father. Master came outside when it was over, He laughed loud when He saw all the bugs lined up in rows as I had asked them to do.

    On the way back home Master told me we were going on a short journey in the morning. I couldn't keep my tail still when I heard that. This means chasing rocks and some serious bug herding. The people we were to see were His age and also very interested in learning all they could about the Great Father. Come to think of it, I need to tell all my animal friends about the Father. I bet some of them would listen and understand.

The sun was almost up when we left the village the next morning. I chased bugs and retrieved rocks for over half the day when I began to tire and decided to just walk next to Master. He never gets tired.

I love it when Master leans down and scratches the top of my head while we walk; that means He has Love for me and that's when I pull on His hand with my mouth and Master laughs and then I laugh too, but my laughs come out as a sharp, loud, noise.

CHAPTER FIVE

Water

~~~

The sun was now a little bit behind us when I noticed that up ahead the ground was shiny and a familiar smell was in the air. Master looked down and smiled at me and said, "I guess you've never seen this before, have you?" He pointed and said "go ahead and see what it is."

I began to run ahead and all of a sudden I couldn't believe what I was seeing. There was water all over the ground. There was so much of it! The only water I'd known came from a dark hole in the ground at the village. The water was everywhere.

Master put down His satchel and walked into the water, kneeled and began splashing the sacred stuff all over His face, hair and robes. Master called me to come to Him; I didn't know if I wanted to do this or not.

I began walking into the thing Master called the Sea of Galilee – the water was very deep – all the way up to my chest! "Look at all this water!" I said to Master. He said "yes, Halo, our Father in heaven gives us wonderful things like this and our food and our friends – everything that is good in this world is of our Father's Love for us."

This water is really something. Master splashed me and I splashed Him back; He fell backwards and I jumped on Him. He then rolled me over on my back, grabbed my front paws and pulled me around in circles. Wow! I wonder if anyone else knows of all this water on the ground.

When we left the place where all the water was, we began to dry out and I realized that I felt different than I felt before I got in the water. Master said that what I felt was cleanliness, that also was given to us by our Father in heaven.

CHAPTER SIX

A New Friend

~~~

The sun was at the top of the hill when we got to the village of Master's friends. His friends are wonderful people. They all wanted to pet me and scratch my head at once. I could get used to this treatment! Master and me were served something to eat and after eating Master and the Guys quietly talked so I decided on a nap.

When I awoke it was morning at the new village and Master and the Guys were already talking among themselves. I wandered outside into the middle of the village and met a new animal friend. She was smaller than me and prettier than me too. I told her about my village and the people there. She had never heard about our Father in heaven or the work that Master and the Guys were doing to spread the word about Love and all that.

She lost interest quickly and wanted to learn how to chase bugs, so I showed her how to catch a bug and not hurt it. She caught on fast; she was very gentle with the bugs not to hurt them. It wasn't long till her other animal friends came around and joined in the bug game. I was surprised that not one bug was injured in all of our fun. I should thank the Father for that one.

The next morning I awoke early and said good-bye to my new

little animal friend as me and Master set off for home. Before long we were at the place where the water was on the ground. I quickly ran into the water and called Master to come play. He declined the soaking but did refill His water bag and rested while I chased the bugs that lived under the water. In no time at all I jumped out of the water, shook and said to Master "I'm clean."

We walked on all day, enjoying each other's company and chasing a few bugs along the way. The more I learn about this Love thing from Master, the more I want to tell my other animal friends so they can feel the way I do.

CHAPTER SEVEN

Love

~~~

One hot afternoon me and Big Friend were lying in the weeds beside the road just outside the village, talking about this thing called Love. I think Big Friend is beginning to understand Love because he said he feels something for the children in the village and I jumped up and said "ya hoo, that's it Big Friend; you do understand!" All of a sudden Big Friend's ears perked up and then I heard it. I heard the sound of many feet tromping on the road.

Big Friend said to me, "those are the bad men; they sometimes hurt the people in the village and take food and other things without asking. I hate them. I tried biting one on the foot one time after he pushed a child to the ground and took her loaf of bread. He kicked me on my side and it hurt for many days. I want them dead, they're evil."

I'd never seen Big Friend be this way and it scared me. We walked well behind these men and followed them into the village. Big Friend said this is good, they didn't even stop; they tromped right on through the village on their way towards the big hill. Big Friend told me never to go near the bad men. I told him I wouldn't.

That evening I told Master about the bad men that me and Big Friend saw. Master said those were soldiers from a far away place called Rome. He said Big Friend was right about staying away from them, but that he was wrong to hate them; we need to love them as we love everything that the Father has made. Master said if we love them, that soon they won't be mean to people anymore.

Well, now I'm really confused, but I'll do as Master says. He hasn't been wrong so far. The next time I see the soldiers, I'll try to love them really hard from a distance.

I really enjoy sitting next to Master near the well in the village and hearing Him teach others about Love and good things and the Father in heaven and how they all should treat each other as they want to be treated. All the animals that live in the village seem to love each other. We never have bad feelings toward each other. I guess that's why animals are different from people. Big Friend tells me that those huge animals with the long ears are special because they carry things for people and are able to move the wooden boxes with wheels. I'm beginning to see that all animals have a place and a job to do. I suppose that's true for people too. Well, it does make sense – if the Father in heaven made them, then every animal and every person is special. Maybe I should teach like Master does. Animals don't seem to want to gather in groups and listen to one animal talk to them; they would rather all talk at once and when that happens, none of them make any sense at all.

CHAPTER EIGHT

Saved

~~~

It was late at night and Master was reading the scrolls by lamplight and I lay on His feet to keep them warm. I was almost asleep when I heard a very faint, tiny scratching noise at the door. I perked up and said to Master "We have company at the door." As I walked toward it, Master opened the door and there sat the tiniest, furry little creature I'd ever seen.

With a tiny little voice, this animal said "hurry, hurry your Big Friend needs you now, bring Master." My insides were pounding and my senses were alert as Master and I followed this tiny creature at a brisk walk; this little fur ball was running all out. When finally we found Big Friend, he was lying down and breathing very roughly. Then I saw it; he had a hole in his side just behind his shoulder. This was horrible; there was wetness coming from the hole. I became very scared. Master scooped up Big Friend in His arms, turned and headed for home. Master said, "Halo, run ahead and wake the Great Lady, we'll need Her help" I ran as fast as I've ever run in my life; water was streaming from my eyes and my nose; I've never been so scared.

The Great Lady jumped from Her bed and put a pot of water over the fire. Master walked in carrying Big Friend and laid him in the place where I sleep, next to the fire. Great Lady began cleaning his side as Master talked to our Father in heaven in a very low, slow voice. White cloth covered the hole now and Master's hand never left his side and he was breathing clearly now.

"Thank you, Halo and thank you, Master" said Big Friend. The darkness had gone away. The sun was coming up; Master lifted His hand off of the cloth and removed the cloth from Big Friend's side. To my relief, the hole in his side was gone. Great Lady gave some food to me and Big Friend and we went slowly outside to sit in the shade for most of the day. I didn't have to ask Master about what happened; Big Friend had been healed by our Father in heaven and His Love for all living things. Big Friend seemed to understand too; his eyes and mine had water in them again, but for a different reason. I said to Big Friend that we were feeling that thing that Master calls "Love." He said we should tell all the other animals about the Love thing.

I turned to Big Friend and asked him who the tiny creature was that came to the door last night. "Oh, just a little friend that comes out of the ground and visits me when you're not around to talk to. His name is "Peep." We must tell Peep "thank you" for his help, I said. "Yea, he did good, didn't he? He sure did."

As we parted that evening, I said to Big Friend, "Hey, how about we chase some bugs in the morning?" "How about you chase 'em and I'll watch ya? Okay?" "I love you, Big Friend." "....I love you too, Halo."

When I got home I ran and jumped in Master's lap and licked His face. He said "I know, Halo, I know. I'm happy to help."

CHAPTER NINE

Giving

~~~

Master is beginning to travel throughout the region, teaching and talking to people about our Father in heaven. I'm very glad that He had asked me to go with Him. I'm learning that there are so very many different kinds of people who need to know the Father and when they do come to know Him their lives change greatly for the better.

Along the way some people travel with us and help to sustain our cause; Master had come to know some of them very well; they have become good friends and very good at scratching my head and my back. All I have to do is walk up to one of them and put my foot on their foot, and I get scratched. When I get home I'll have to show Big Friend this new trick; he likes being scratched too.

I've learned to really enjoy eating bread and fish every day; it seems that is what most people eat when they travel. Every day there is new scenery to look at. This place we live in is really something special

Even with all the traveling we do, Master still goes home to help His other father make things for people and to build houses in many different villages. Master's family is very important to Him. There is much Love between them all.

I really enjoy going back home to see my friends; they never change. My favorite of all is Big Friend; he will always be my closest animal friend 'cause we know what Love is.

Master has told me that some day we will journey to a very large place called a city where there is this building called a temple. This temple thing is where the essence of the Heavenly

Father lives and many people go there from all over to visit Him; but Master told me I still can't go inside. He said I could probably talk to the Father just as easily from outside the building. Anyway, Master said there would be plenty of bugs there to keep out of the temple that would probably keep me busy all day.

Master, His earth father and me went on a journey to fix the roof of a house of a woman with many children. My job was to keep the children out of the house while it was being repaired. I have so much fun when playing with little people. They know only Love and give it away to everyone, especially to animals. It was half a day before the roof was fixed and the children could return back inside. The woman handed Earth Father a sack with grain in it, but he wouldn't take it. He hugged her and we left for home.

I said to Master, we could make bread with that sack of grain; the Great Lady makes good bread. "I know, Halo, but the woman whose roof we fixed could also make bread with it; and, her children, I'm sure, enjoy her bread at dinner time." "I understand, Master, it's that Love thing again, isn't it?" "Yes, Halo, that's what it is; we must always help one another when help is needed. That way no one is left behind." "I love you, Master." "I know, Halo, I love you too."

CHAPTER TEN

The Toad

~~~

Earth Father picked up a rock and threw it far up ahead and said "bring it, Halo. Bring it back." I was off with the speed of a bird. I couldn't find the rock that earth father threw; so I picked up one that looked like it and he never knew the difference. Master knew it was the wrong rock, but didn't say anything; He just winked at me and smiled.

Master must have taught the rock game to Earth Father, because he seemed to really enjoy tossing rocks up the road and watching me wear myself out chasing them. I thought I would trick Earth Father; so after he threw a rock up the road and into the weeds and I ran after it, I saw a toad near the rock, so I gently picked it up and laid it at Earth Father's feet. He and Master laughed so hard they had to sit down and rest. They thought that was real cute of me, but I just needed a break from the rock game. I lay on Master's feet with my tongue hanging out.

Some of my animal friends herd sheep and goats for their masters; I suppose they enjoy that. I don't think I would like it or be good at it; I really don't like goats or sheep 'cause they're not very smart at all. If they were smart, you could call them and they would come running to you; but, no, they just stand there with a far-off look in their eyes, chewing on whatever it is they chew on. I can't imagine chewing on anything for that long a time; maybe it's rocks they chew on.

Speaking of chewing, as we neared the house, we were met by Great Lady and she had hugs and plates of food for us when we came through the door.

I really enjoy being a part of this family; they treat me like I am one of them. I don't think any other animals have it this good. I think the Father gave them to me. "Thank You, Father."

Today Big Friend told me about the new family that he is living with. They came here to Nazareth about two weeks ago, after the bad men with funny clothes burned their house down and took all they owned. Big Friend said they are very glad to be in our village where the people care for one another. Their new house is small but built much better than the old house far away. They had an animal friend with them and Big Friend now has a friend and a family to sleep with at night.

I was through playing for the day and was tired and thirsty. I hopped over the door sill and ran for my bowl and drank deeply. Father made a real good thing when He made water, but I wish the women at the well wouldn't argue over it; that's just silly!

"Halo, come over here; I have something to tell you." "Hi, Master, I missed you today." "Thank you, Halo; what I have to tell you is sad, but wonderful. My earth father has left us to go be with our Father in heaven and he won't be back ever again in his earthly body, but his spirit will live forever." "Oh, Master, that's wonderful, when can we go and be with the Heavenly Father?" "We will have to wait a while, Halo; our time has not come yet. When it is time, we will see Joseph again." "You're right, Master, it's sad Earth Father didn't scratch my chin and say goodbye before he left." "Well, Halo, we can't always say goodbye before we leave." "I'll say goodbye to you, Master, before I leave." "I'm sure you will, Halo, I'm sure you will."

Master has taken the place of Earth Father and become the head of the family. He will do a very good job at this, I'm sure. The Great Lady still won't let me sleep on Earth Father's bed; she says it's not right for an animal to sleep in a bed. I think she's wrong, but I always do what I'm asked. Master taught me that.

CHAPTER ELEVEN

Shorty

~~~

Big friend's new animal friend is very small, no bigger than a loaf of bread; and he squeeks when he talks. Big Friend and me call him "Shorty" because of his size. I thought that was quite clever. Shorty is now a regular with me and Big Friend. He goes everywhere we go. Shorty is very good at chasing bugs unlike Big Friend. Big Friend would rather watch the action than to join in.

Shorty was happy to meet Master and said that He was much different than any people he had ever met before. He said he felt very safe when he was near Master. I said, "yea that's the way I feel too."

Master and I were playing the rock game one day when Shorty ran up and wanted to play, so Master chose smaller rocks for Shorty and he did very well. After a time Shorty ran back with a shiny, round, yellow metal thing and dropped it at Master's feet. Master said, "Well, well Shorty, you just made quite a find here." He looked it over closely and smiled at Shorty.

"Now Shorty, put this in your mouth and don't drop it. I want you to take this home and give to the head of your household. Go now, and don't stop until it's delivered safely. Halo, you go with Shorty and make sure the deed is done." "OK, Master."

We arrived at Shorty's house and Shorty dropped the yellow metal thing at the feet of his earth father, who started jumping up and down and laughing. He picked up Shorty and kissed and hugged him.

I guess Master knew what He was doing, because Shorty's earth father became so happy he cried and so did his earth mother. I wonder where I can find a round, yellow metal thing. Shorty and I returned to the rock game with Master with no luck at finding any more shiny things.

CHAPTER TWELVE

Soldiers

~~~

Master and I left home the following morning on an extended journey to see more friends who live by the Sea of Galilee. They're the ones who collect fish out of the water and use them for food. I was able to play in the water briefly while Master studied scrolls with his friends. I found some children to play with in the water, but they're not near as much fun to play with as Master is. He just has a way of making me happy when we play together. As I began to dry out, I felt that clean feeling again. That's a gift from the Father in Heaven; I should do this more often, but the sea is the only water big enough for me to jump into and play.

Master and I stayed with His friends for many days and just before leaving, He stood on a hillside and spoke to many, many people concerning the Heavenly Father. They listened closely and were very quiet while Master spoke; some even cried. I don't know why though, maybe they found a shiny yellow metal, round thing and that made them happy.

I think these people love Master, because of the way they act toward Him. I'm not sure anyone could love Master as I do though.

When we left that village by the sea, some people came with us carrying blankets and food to our next stop on our journey. After a while, a small yellow and black bird flew down and landed on Masters shoulder and began talking bird talk very excitedly to Him. I don't understand bird talk very well, because I never get to practice with the birds; they're either flying or up in a tree. I just can't reach 'em.

Master told everyone to get off the road and hide behind the rocks and trees to the right of the road. I lay silently beside Master and soon, here came the soldiers from Rome marching past, raising dust and clanking loudly like cook pots banging together. After some minutes, our group came from behind the rocks and trees and we continued our journey. Master told everyone to avoid the soldiers whenever possible. He said lack of contact means lack of trouble. That's kind of the way Big Friend described it to me the first time I'd ever seen them back in Nazareth; that's our village we live in.

When I think of our village, I begin missing Big Friend and Shorty and, of course, the Great Lady and all the little kids in the village. But I'm happy to be here with Master and His friends who are following along. As we rested in the middle of the day, Master's friends were asking questions one after another about Heaven and our Father who resides there. Master reminded them all that our Heavenly Father is everywhere, all the time and that they can call on His help any time, anywhere. Master had the perfect answer for every question asked by the group. He was teaching them slowly but effectively over time so they didn't miss a thing. Like the way He taught me how to chase bugs and bring back rocks to Him, when I was little. It took almost two days to learn the rock game.

I think the Father in Heaven is probably very pleased with Master for being such a wonderful teacher of men and animals alike. I must be the most fortunate animal in the world, to be Master's very close friend.

As the day ended and the sun was low, we walked away from the road for a way and a fire was made behind some big rocks. Blankets were spread closely together and food was passed around for all. Master and me always share a blanket to stay warm at night. As Master taught, I began dozing off on the blanket near the fire, listening to His sweet voice and the questions from the group.

After a while, I felt Master lie down beside me and put His arm around me and pull me close to Him. The fire went low and crackled softly as we dozed off to sleep. Master was probably thinking of the Father in heaven, but I was thinking of chasing bugs, retrieving rocks and just being with Big Friend and Shorty. I can hear people snoring gently.

I was the first to wake in the morning. Yawning and stretching was the first thing I did and breathing in Master's ear came next. He brushed His ear and kept sleeping; I breathed in His ear again and He brushed His ear again. Next I got nose to nose with Him; His eyes came open slightly and I began licking His face as fast as my tongue would work. He and I were laughing and rolling on the blanket like two children playing. It ended with Master giving me a good scratch under my chin and a back rub that lasted over a minute.

After having some food, we set out again; some of Master's students went a different direction than us or maybe they went back home. Whatever the case, it's nice having so many for company when we travel.

Two people were left walking with me and Master; as he spoke to them, I walked behind sniffing in the bushes for any bugs to chase; not many out this early in the morning, I guess.

Soon the other two travelers departed and set out in another direction and Master and I were alone together again – oh, yea – and the Heavenly Father – He's always with us. Master says no one makes it very far without the Father above looking after His people and animals.

I wonder if wild animals and bugs understand about the Heavenly Father and how important He is to living a good life.

CHAPTER THIRTEEN

Big Friend Leaves

~~~

Days later Master and I returned to the village only to find out that Big Friend had left to go live with the Father in Heaven. Shorty said that Big Friend wanted him to say goodbye for him; he said we would meet up later and have forever to continue our friendship.

I was sad at first, but then remembered I'll see Joseph, the earth father, and Big Friend in heaven to talk to or play with; but he's safe with the Father now and I'm happy for that.

Meanwhile, Shorty is jumping around in circles wanting to go play with the children of the village. I don't know if I can keep up with Shorty, but I'm trying. Now I understand why Big Friend wanted to just watch when I was chasing bugs and retrieving rocks when I was younger. Shorty is so cute. He brings the bugs to me as if I were collecting them for a later date. I just tell them to run away and shoo them off. Shorty doesn't even notice that they're gone; he has a lot of fun running back and forth. I know how he feels; you get a great feeling of accomplishment after catching a multitude of bugs or chasing rock after rock while Master laughs and thinks I'm silly for bringing them back to Him. Some day I would like to learn to throw rocks for Shorty; I know he would enjoy that game.

Master has been working very hard lately to make up for Earth Father being gone. We miss him very much, but we understand that being with the Heavenly Father is a beautiful place to be.

Shorty has become a wonderful friend but he's nothing like Big Friend was. Master told me once that no two animals or people are the same; and He sure was right about that. I'm glad I have the sense not to jump around in circles all day like Shorty; I just know people talk about him.

CHAPTER FOURTEEN

The Scarf

~~~

The Great Lady, Master's Mother, and I went to the well in
the middle of the village today for water. There was a commotion
at the well; it seems a woman dropped her headscarf into the well.
To her, it was very valuable because it was a gift from her children.
Great Lady sent me to find Shorty and I knew right away what she
had in mind. I found Shorty at his home begging for food.

Shorty and I ran to the well with haste. When we arrived,
the Great Lady put Shorty in the bucket attached to the rope and
lowered him down into the dark hole. When the bucket was pulled
back up, there was Shorty with a soggy headscarf in his mouth and
his tail going back and forth very fast.

Shorty saved the day; that little guy was nothing but smiles all day long; he even got some bone scraps from the scarf lady and he shared with me.

Shorty has a big heart for a little fellow. Everywhere we went for the next few days, Shorty was treated like a hero and was given many scratches on his back and under his chin. I even got some of the overflow.

Master did explain to Shorty that the Father in Heaven makes good things like that happen and happen for a reason. I don't know if Shorty was listening or not; he was so busy bouncing up and down in circles.

CHAPTER FIFTEEN

John
~~~

We're leaving tomorrow on a journey to go see a friend of Master's named John. He lives next to a thing called Jordan. Master says He is very smart and knows the teachings of the Father better than most people. He sounds like Master; Master knows many very interesting people and a lot of smart ones too.

I'm going to teach John the rock game when I meet Him. I know He'll like it just like Master does. Not everybody can play the rock game the right way though; some throw the rock far into the weeds and I can't find it, or they don't try; they just toss it in front of me and expect me to have fun by picking it up and handing it to them with my mouth.

The more I hear from Master about this friend, John, the more excited I am to see Him. He sounds like a good friend to me already. The one thing I find to be very odd is that He eats bugs whereas I chase them. Eating bugs seems like something a bird would do. Oh, well, as long as He plays the rock game and knows the Heavenly Father, He's OK by me.

When Master and I arrived, John was sitting near water with a few people around Him. Master said this water was called Jordan. I was the first in the water and playing by myself when Master and John came in to also play. When Master went under the water, I jumped on Him and fell over backwards when He came back up. Master pushed me towards the edge and I climbed out. When I turned around I shook the water off and was surprised to see a beautiful light shining on Master and for the first time I heard what I think was the Heavenly Father saying nice things to Master.

From this time on, Master seemed more wonderful than ever before. I asked Master what had happened and He said, a very important event had just happened and that I wouldn't understand it's complexity. Master is right; when He uses words like complexity, He's lost me!

John and me, we played the rock game for a while, but I could tell that John wasn't interested in continuing the game, so I was content to watch the other people play with John in the water.

Master seemed even wiser and more able to communicate with the Father after playing in Jordan with His friend, John.

A crowd gathered around Master that evening as we ate. I recognized a few of the Guys from other journeys we went on. They were glad to see me 'cause I got scratches from all of them, and they didn't even notice me coming around a second time for more scratches. After a while their low voices put me to sleep. Master rested His hand on my head; there is no better feeling than that.

In the morning I awoke to Master breathing in my ear. I was up and licking His face in no time. Master said goodbye to John and we were off into the desert.

CHAPTER SIXTEEN

Grape Juice

~~~

Master and me walked for days and days wandering back and forth, going here and there. Then one afternoon a bad thing approached us and made me growl; but Master was strong and made the bad thing go away, with the help of our Father in Heaven. We walked on for many, many days. Master did not eat and that bothered me. I ate what I could find and got by.

After so many days in the wilderness, we finally came to a village where we rested and ate food. Master did well for going so long without eating; and drinking very little. He is very strong, to journey away for so long.

Master and I traveled for a while to another village and He healed some people who didn't feel well. As we began to leave that village, five Guys joined us in our travels. It's always exciting to have Master's friends near, because of the constant talk of the Father's Love for all living things; but no one knows more of this than Master; He seems to be teaching the new teachers of this Love thing. I feel special to be here with the Guys and being in the middle of so much Love.

Today we all went to a big party with many people, all dressed in very special clothes and eating lots of food. As people would drop food on the ground, I would clean it up for them. I said to Master that we should attend more parties like this one. He warned me of the excess of food and I agreed; my tummy was swollen and round. Just before I went to a corner for a nap, Master was praised for making grape juice from pots of water. I suspect the Heavenly Father had a hand in that one. Master said the party would have gone bad and ended without the grape juice. I'll take water over grape juice any day.

Later in the evening, Master woke me and said it was time to say goodbye and go to our camp a short ways away. When we got there Master and the Guys built fire and began discussing the scrolls. I was content to lie back down with Master's hand on my head and doze off again.

Master is right about the excess of food; I'd never eaten so much before. Master says to experience all things in moderation and keep greed at bay. I believe I learned a lesson tonight; I won't need to eat for days.

Over the last week, we traveled to where the big water is in the Galilee. Master had a crowd around Him the whole time, with people wanting to know about the Father and the scrolls. The Guys are also helping to teach people; that makes Master's job easier.

The people who catch fish from the water are wonderful people. They love Master and listen to all He talks about and they feed us fish and bread when we need it. I've learned to eat little bits at a time since the big party we were at. While we were at the big water, Master healed many people and made much happiness for the people who live there. He was showered with gifts from all sides. When the gifting stopped, Master instructed the Guys to gather up all the gifts and pass them out to all the very poor people in the village. What a wonderful person Master is. He's teaching all the people He talks to, to be like Himself and love all that they come into contact with; even the ones they don't like. Most people find that difficult. I find it easy to love everyone because Master taught me the right way to live in this life according to the laws of our Heavenly Father.

Master told me that the Father has given His people ten rules to follow for living a good life. Master said some of those rules have rubbed off on me. That's good to know. Master makes me feel so special. I love Him more than I can ever express.

CHAPTER SEVENTEEN

Back to Life

~~~

As we travel toward our village, I think about the Great Lady and miss Her soft voice, Her chin scratches and the bread She bakes. I also miss Shorty and the children. In a day or so we'll be back home chasing bugs, jumping around with Shorty and playing with all those cute little kids.

Master and I have been together now for many, many years and have been on many journeys together. He has taught many people about the scrolls and the Heavenly Father. Master said we were chosen to spread the word and I'm so proud to be part of Master's mission.

Master said my fifteenth birthday is coming up soon and we should have a party. I said OK, if I don't eat too much, like I did last time. The day rolled around and Master invited Shorty and my other animal friends and the kids in the village to join in the fun. We ran, we played, chased bugs, retrieved rocks, bounced in circles and ate scraps that Master collected for us animals. What a wonderful party we had that day. I believe all the animals and children went to bed early that evening because we were so worn out. The next morning, I didn't feel any older, but I guess I'm not supposed to.

Master has been going on some journeys without me because He needs me to stay home with the family and protect them and the rest of the village; but He never fails to return to me and tell me all about what He did with the Guys. There's nine of them now, plus Master. They're all becoming quite popular in Galilee.

Recently, I traveled with Master to a place called Jerusalem; a large town full of people and many of them needing Master's help to heal them of sickness. Master said to let them pet me because it would make them feel better while they waited for their healing from Master. The Guys help to heal people too; they had learned well from Master.

We walked up on a man sitting in water with bent legs; he could not walk and hadn't walked for years, he said. The crowd of people that had been following us stepped back and was silent as Master walked into the water and kneeled in front of him. There came a beautiful light for a moment and Master commanded the man to rise and to walk from the pool. I wanted to jump into the pool to celebrate and play, but one of the Guys held me back and the man stood and walked from the pool directly to Master and hugged Him tightly and wept. Most all the people there had tears in their eyes. Master walked for a way with His arm around the man and soon the man walked off into the crowd without even a limp.

Our journey is now leading us to a mountain where more of Master's friends waited for Him to arrive. Master talked to crowds of people over a few days and healed people who felt bad. By the time we left the mountain, we had twelve Special Guys in our group. I'll never run out of hugs and scratches at this rate.

On we traveled for a day and a half, before we stopped at a village where a poor woman's son had left to be with the Father; but she said it was too soon for him to leave her alone. Master went right into the house where the boy lay and asked everyone to leave. When the house was empty, I perked up my ears and could hear Master reciting the scrolls and talking to the Father. This went on for a time and then I could hear two voices softly talking to the Father. A while later, Master and the woman's son walked through the door of the home and again I could see the beautiful light shining down on the two of them.

The woman cried and hugged her son tightly. Master waved His hand over them, said goodbye and we were again on our way down a dusty road to a house where we were invited to eat and stay the night. Everyone wants Master and me and the Guys to stop and eat with them, 'cause we're well known everywhere we go. This house where we ate was large and there were many people there for dinner; they all wanted to talk to Master at once but He made them all take their turn with Him. Just before bedtime, a woman came to the door and ran straight for Master; she began wiping Master's feet with her hair. I thought this to be very odd; I couldn't understand why she used her hair to clean Master's feet, but Master thought it to be gracious and respectful to Him. It wasn't long after that I was asleep by the fire next to Master.

CHAPTER EIGHTEEN

Miracles

~~~

A few days later, we arrived at the place of the big water; Master and the Guys and me were on our way across the water in what Master called a boat. It was very strange to be on the water and not getting wet. We needed to go all the way across this water to the hills to heal a person who has waited for us for quite a while; it sounded important to me.

I wasn't too sure about floating on the water in this thing called a boat to start with, but when the sky darkened and the wind began to blow, I became frightened and began to shake uncontrollably. I asked Master if there was something He could do to stop this scary situation. I leaned firmly on Master's leg to steady myself. Soon, Master stood up and stretched out His arms and asked the Father in Heaven to calm the waters and give us safe passage; in a moment, the boat stopped tossing, the wind quit blowing so hard and the rain stopped.

I stopped shaking and then turned to see the most beautiful sunset I'd ever seen; the edge of the water was brilliant orange, purple and red. By the time we reached the other side of the big water and left the boat, the stars were out and shining brighter than I'd ever seen them. I'm not often frightened by anything, but that boat scared me a lot. Master scratched my head and told me that the Father has all things in His Hand and, when asked, will make all things good and perfect.

The boat ride back to the other side wasn't near as scary as the ride over, but I'm still not looking forward to the next time I climb onto a boat.

From village to village we all traveled; Master and the twelve Guys we're traveling with are healing all the people we meet. I sure enjoy traveling with the Guys. I'm never without someone to play with at any time of day. I've learned when not to bother

Master for playtime. He's busy most of the time now with healing people and teaching. I just know the Father in Heaven is very proud of Master.

Not long after the boat ride, we arrived at a large valley between two hills where Master spoke to the largest crowd of people I'd ever seen; they covered the hills on both sides and most of the valley.

Master spoke for quite a while and then decided to break for something to eat. Well, everyone there but us forgot their lunch. Can you imagine that? No one brought food with them. Leave it to our Father and Master to take care of everyone's needs. Master held up a loaf of bread and some fish to the Heavens; then He placed them in baskets to be passed around to the huge crowd of people. The baskets of bread and fish seemed to never get empty; more baskets appeared with more fish and bread until everyone had been fed and wanted no more to eat. That one was even better than making the wind, rain and clouds go away on the scary boat ride.

It was very odd that the bread I ate tasted just like the bread the Great Lady makes back in our village. I looked around expecting to see Her making Her famous bread, but didn't see Her; and the fish was just like the fish the Guys would gather out of the big water and sell to people. What a wonderful day this turned out to be. The people on the hills cheered Master and the Guys for serving the meal. Master told them to remember to thank the Father every day for making their lives so good. There was a silence as everyone bowed their heads and said "thank you." I bowed my head too, and when I did, I caught sight of a bug and took off running after it. I guess the Father blesses me with bugs to chase, I like that; it keeps me from becoming bored or lazy. Master chuckled when He saw me run after the bug and said "that's my Halo." I stopped and looked up and said "that's my Master."

Master spoke for a while longer to the people on the hills and we then left to go to our camp where a fire was lit and blankets were spread. The Guys were very tired from the day's work but Master never gets tired of teaching. He says the Father gives Him all the strength He needs to carry on through the day. Maybe that's why I have so much energy all day long. The Father is taking very good care of me, even at my age.

In the middle of the night we had to leave our camp because of all the people coming to see Master. The Guys got the boat ready and we all climbed in, except for Master; He wanted to walk around the water and meet us on the other side of the big water. I wasn't too wild about another boat trip, but I didn't have a choice. The water was rough and the going was slow but we were making headway. About halfway into our boat ride the Guys spotted a figure in the distance through the water clouds, walking on top of the water; the Guys were very frightened of this but I could tell it was Master and He was calling one of the Guys to join Him. He said "have faith, you can do it." I thought to myself "this probably won't work," but without questioning, one of the Guys stepped out of the boat and began walking toward Master slowly – on top of the water. I wondered if I could do that too, but Master told me to stay. I obeyed and watched Master's friend slowly approach Master; suddenly he disappeared, falling straight through the water and began swimming the way I do.

Master reached down and picked his friend out of the water and slowly walked to the boat with him. Once Master and his friend were in the boat, it wasn't long before we were on the dirt again. I've had about enough of boats for a while. We made another camp not far away and all went to sleep; me in Master's arms.

Our journey from the big water led us very far away. We walked for days, most of the time there was no road to follow. This was hard on the Guys; their feet became sore after four straight days of walking without a road. Master and me, we didn't have a problem for some reason.

We stopped at a place where there was a pool of water and rested for a day. Master suggested to the Guys that they heal each others' feet of their soreness and let the Father in Heaven have glory in this.

Soon the Guys were all sitting in a circle healing the feet of the person on their left. I looked at Master; He looked at me; we softly laughed under our breath. This was quite a site to see. It wasn't long before the Guys all had new feet to walk on and they thanked Master for the good idea.

CHAPTER NINTEEN

A Cross

~~~

We were on our way again the next morning. Later I sniffed something in the air; I ran ahead of the group and saw a village over the next large hill and ran back to tell Master. He stopped the Guys and told them to rest, while I went to the village to see if it was safe to enter. When I returned, I told Master I thought it was safe to enter the village.

Master found a woman He was seeking along with her daughter, who was very ill. Master wanted me to stay close to her and let her pet me while He healed her. It wasn't long before me and the little girl were outside playing the rock game. She was a beautiful little girl and she could run fast too. Her mother made food for us all, as we made camp that night next to her house. The food was different, but tasted good. The people here talked differently also, but we understood them.

These people in this village had no idea who the Father in Heaven was, so Master and the Guys got right to work teaching this village about the scrolls and our Heavenly Father. This took two days work for them, but it gave me time to play with the children and search for some interesting bugs to chase. This village didn't have any animals like me to play with; just some goats and sheep and a very old camel. None of them knew how to play, so I avoided them. They just stand around chewing on stuff. I wonder what it is they chew on.

Master said we taught the village well; He was happy with the outcome and the little girl was healed and is now healthy and happy. We left the village in the morning and this time we had a road to walk on. I heard some of the Guys thanking the Father for the road and healthy feet to walk on. I never have a problem with sore feet. Neither does Master; I suppose we have Heavenly feet given to us by the Father.

Master said we now had a long way to travel to our next village. Master leaned down and scratched my head. I can't reach Master's head.

It was a very hot, dry journey to our next village to teach about the Father. Master and the Guys seemed very happy on this journey; they laughed and joked around most of the way and I wore myself out chasing rocks and bugs the whole way.

As we arrived at the village, we could see that the bad men with funny clothes and hats had recently been there and had caused trouble for the people. Fires burned in a couple of the houses and a man was hung up high and nailed to some wood. I couldn't look because it scared me too much. Master told me to go into the weeds and play with the children and chase some bugs. I led a group of children away to play the rock game and after a while when we returned, the man on the wood was gone and Master was washing His hands in a bucket with some of the Guys.

I guess Master fixed everything the way He always does. When I asked Master about the man, Master said the Father had everything and everyone placed where they should be. Master stopped and made loving thought to the bad men and then we began making our camp within the walls of the village. This village had a well that looked like the one in our village, but the water in it wasn't as good tasting as our water; ours tasted cold and sweet. I love our village and the people in it. I can't wait to see them again and Shorty too.

We went to a home where a man and woman lived and had some food; it was very tasty from under the table where I found plenty. After dinner, Master healed the man who could not hear or speak. Master put His hands on the man's head and spoke to the Father; when He was finished, the man said, "thank you, Rabbi" and his wife started to weep with joy and love for Master. Again Master refused the shiny, yellow metal things presented to Him. Master said the glory goes to the Father in Heaven. We stayed in this village for days. It was a nice place to stay where the people loved us and the children knew right where to scratch me on the head and under my chin.

Master and the Guys went to a large hill outside of the village and spoke to a very, very large crowd of people. Most came from other villages in the region. Master talked to them for a long while and again all these people forgot their lunch and Master wanted to feed them. Again Master multiplied the fish and bread to make enough to feed all of these people and have enough left over to fill several baskets. Many people were healed that day and all were given the message from Master about using Love to make their lives better and to thank the Father for the good life given to them. I thank the Father every day, just like Master told me to do. I'm proof that, thanking the Father leads to a good life.

In the weeks to follow, we went on more boat rides and saw many villages. I still don't like boat rides so much; I'd rather walk in the dust on a road any day.

CHAPTER TWENTY

Lepers

~~~

After a few days, we came to a huge hill and Master, me and three of the Guys went to the top of this huge hill and there we saw the bright light shine on Master and two people were there with us. This was very pretty to me. Then the Father spoke and I was amazed at what I heard - He said Master was His son and the two new Guys left and went away. When we left the hill and came down to the others, not a word was said about what happened. A crowd waited for us as we joined the rest of the Guys.

Out of the crowd a man came and asked Master to heal his boy who made screeching sounds, fell to the ground and white stuff was all over his face. I felt sorrow for the little boy and went to comfort him when Master grabbed my tail and pulled me back and said, "not yet Halo." The Guys had tried to heal the boy, but couldn't. Master took a cloth and wiped the boy's mouth clean and He picked the boy up in His arms and cradled him. Master said something about "Be Gone!" and the boy was healed to perfection. The crowd was amazed at the healing and knew it was the Father that brought about the healing.

We were on our way again to a village where there were ten men who had things on their faces and hands and needed to be healed. When we got near the village, they yelled something to Master and Master told the ten men to go. When they did so, they were healed of the ugly things on their bodies. One of the men came back to Master, knelt and thanked Him for the healing; the others walked away.

Master knows that the people who are healed are thankful to Him and the Father. He wants all people to praise the Father in Heaven because that's where all Love starts from and ends up. Master sure has a way with words; I'm very glad we can under-stand each others' thoughts, but I guess Master knows everyone's thoughts.

We had traveled again for many days to reach the home of one of Master's good friends. When we arrived at the house, Master found His friend's sisters crying. Master's friend had left to be with the Father in Heaven. His name was Lazarus. The sisters didn't want him to live with the Father yet and asked if Master might help them bring him back.

Master, me and the Guys went to a large hole in the rocks where Master's friend Lazarus' earth body lay; the hole was exposed and Master said, "come out, Lazarus and be with us." Out walked a man covered in rags and smelling badly. He needed to go to the big water and clean himself like me and Master do.

Master's friend walked to Him and hugged Him; the sisters cried and ran to Lazarus and began cleaning the rags from his body, washing him and putting a new robe on him

The Guys were very surprised at what they saw and the crowd of people too; but I see it as quite natural for Master to do these kinds of good things for people. Master's Love for all living things is far greater than that of the people who haven't learned of the Father yet. That's why Master and the Guys work so hard to teach people about this thing called Love. I wish I could help teach the Love thing; but Master says I'm doing my part just as the Father in heaven wants me to do. We had something to eat with Lazarus and his sisters that evening. While everyone talked after our food, I headed toward the fire, lay down and was asleep and dreaming of bugs in a short time.

In the morning, Master, me and the Guys left for another village two days away, but the road was good and spirits were high and I was able to find and bring back every rock that was tossed by the Guys. I don't run after the rocks near as fast as I used to. I find it less tiring to trot to the rocks because they're not going anywhere before I find them. The Guys have taken to putting marks on the rocks to make sure I get the right ones. The Guys can't fool me, but sometimes I fool them, and make them laugh when I bring back a toad instead of the rock that was thrown.

We had come to a place where Master wanted to speak to the crowds who had gathered to hear about the Father in Heaven. As Master began speaking, the Guys shooed away the children who gathered at the front; Master told the Guys that was wrong to do. Master drew all the children up front and close to Him and I was right in the middle of them getting scratches and hugs. The Guys realized it was important for the children to learn early about the Father and not to stand in the way of teaching about Love.

Master was talking, teaching, touching and healing all at the same time; people everywhere say He's the greatest man ever to live. I think so; I knew that a long time ago. I don't know where I would be without Master; I hope He feels the same about me.

Everywhere we go now, huge crowds gather and Master is expected to do wonderful things for people. The Guys help out a lot, but the crowds follow us now from village to village. Master still has time to play the rock game with me and I still seem to find enough bugs to chase. I just chase them a little slower than I used to.

I've been with Master for what seems like forever. I can't imagine being with anyone else for that long; it wouldn't seem right not to spend my life with the greatest man to ever live. I'm the most fortunate animal to ever live. I suppose knowing about Love the way I do, helps me to have the life I enjoy so much. Master has protected me and taught me everything I know. I have a feeling people will be hearing about Master for a long, long time; even after He leaves to go live with the Father in Heaven.

Every time we stop for Master to speak to the people, the crowds get bigger. Each time, learning about Love and the Heavenly Father is spreading very quickly. I know that's what Master wants, because He never takes a break from teaching and talking to the crowds of people on our journeys. I feel that I'm a part of something big, but I'm not sure what it is yet. I'll stick with Master till I figure it out, or maybe I'm not supposed to figure it out. One way or another, me and Master belong together to the end.

CHAPTER TWENTY-ONE

Aging

~~~

    We are only a day away from our village, Nazareth, and I
can't wait to see everybody again. We've been away for quite
a while. I wonder about the Great Lady and all the kids in the
village and I wonder if Shorty has grown any. I wonder if any new
families have moved to our village. Master seemed to be excited
about getting home to our village too; I think He wants to see the
Great Lady. They're very close to each other, just like all children
are to their mothers. But this time seems special for some reason.

Maybe because we've been gone for such a long time. I couldn't imagine being gone from Master for that long a time.

As we neared our village, I saw the Great Lady standing by the well, waving to Master and here comes Shorty running as fast as those short little legs would carry him. Sure enough, when he got to us, he started jumping up and down in circles and squeaking like a bird. It sure was good to see him; we have a lot to catch up on.

Master and the Great Lady hugged and went to the house while the Guys refreshed themselves at the well. Shorty and me rested in the shade while I told him about our travels. Shorty seemed more interested this time; maybe because he's catching on to what we're doing by teaching about Love.

It wasn't long before Shorty and me were out chasing bugs with a couple of his friends. He taught the other animals like us how to chase bugs while I was gone with Master; Shorty and his friends are much faster at bug-chasing than me, but I still have fun at the game. Sometimes I like to just watch the others chase the bugs; they'll bring them to me to show me what wonderful bug chasers they are. Shorty has taught them well; no bugs have been hurt so far as I can tell. I reminded Shorty about being gentle with the bugs, 'cause we don't want to run out of them.

A couple of the Guys and me taught Shorty and his friends how to retrieve rocks; I think they like that game even better than the bug game. They felt a great deal of accomplishment when fetching rocks for the Guys.

It was very hot that night so I slept outside the house on a clump of grass; it was soft like Master's blanket. I could hear all the noises from the bugs and wild animals in the distance. Some of the Guys slept nearby and they made small snorting noises with their noses. I think they do that to keep wild animals away.

As I began to doze off to sleep, I thought about all the places Master and I have seen and the many, many journeys we've been on together; all the people and animals we've met and the ones we've healed. It makes me tired to think about it all now.

I often think about Big Friend and Earth Father living with our Father in Heaven and I miss them a lot but I remember what Master said about seeing them again in Heaven; that will be a wonderful time, I'm sure.

I woke in the morning with Shorty squeaking and rubbing his nose on my nose; he wants to go play with the children in the village and the other animals like us. I rose up, yawned and stretched my legs and followed Shorty to where the children were gathered near the edge of the village. I enjoyed playing for a while, but then I decided to watch for a time. These kids just wear me out! Shorty, being small as he was, could out run any of the children in a dash and the other animals, too. I'm glad to see Shorty keeping an eye on all the children in the village; the Father made that happen.

It's very satisfying to watch Shorty, the other animals and the children all playing together and loving one another. I wonder if our village is special that way; or if all animals and children love each other wherever they are. I believe this Love Thing is much more important than anyone realizes. Master has taught about Love all of my life and probably before I was here to help Him.

The Father and Master have a special way of speaking that I don't understand, but as long as Master lets me know what is said, I can pass it on to the other animals and Shorty. Sometimes I think it's more difficult to teach people about Love than it is to teach the animals. Maybe it's more natural for animals to listen about something so wonderful and important.

The children and the animals have all come over to where I'm sitting and have plopped on the ground, breathing hard and dirty from the dust, they all began to rest in the shade. The children were talking about whatever children usually talk about and Shorty and the other animals were almost asleep and getting a much needed rest from their workout with the kids.

I wonder why children don't chase bugs and run after rocks like me and Shorty. They certainly have the energy for those games; probably for the same reason Shorty and I don't wear robes and eat at a table.

I said goodbye to Shorty and the others and began walking towards the house. Master was there with the Guys, reading the scrolls and talking softly. I went to Master and He knew right away what I was there for; He gave me a good scratching on my head and back. I then went to the Guys and they each gave me some scratches. I wonder why no one gives them scratches. Probably because they can reach their own heads.

CHAPTER TWENTY-TWO

Heavenly Journey

~~~

Master came to me later in the day to explain to me that He, the Great Lady and the Guys would be going on a journey to a place called Jerusalem for a special event; along with most of the people in Nazareth. Only the very old and the very young would stay home.

Master asked that I stay behind and help to protect those remaining at home. He wanted Shorty's and the other animals' help too. He asked me to spread the word that we were in charge of protecting all of those who weren't making the journey. I told Master we would watch them day and night. Master said "Halo, you're a very special animal." I said to Master, "I know."

In the morning, most of the village had packed what they needed and began slowly moving along the road towards the special event. Master hugged me and said "Thank you, Halo; I'll see you later." And with that, Shorty and I watched as they moved down the road and waved goodbye to the people remaining behind.

I gathered Shorty and the other animals and explained what we had to do and all agreed to help protect everyone left in the village. Shorty and the other animals were proud to be chosen to look after the village while so many people left for a few days. I asked that all animals sleep outside and listen for any odd noises at night. I also remembered we had the Father in Heaven to help us with our task.

Lately when I sleep, I have night thoughts of Master and the Guys and wonder if they're having a good time at the big town so far away. Today I lay in the shade a lot and watched the children play with the animals like me and Shorty. The children seem to be made of pure Love and are willing to spread that Love all over the village.

Today, I thought I heard Master's voice, but it wasn't; it was two old men talking by the well. I do wish Master would return home; I miss Him very much.

All has been quiet and safe here in the village for seven days. I think Shorty has everything under control with the other animals; he sure has been a lot of help. I must tell him how much I Love him, when he comes by.

Oh! there's Master's voice again. He's talking to me. "Master, it's wonderful to hear your voice. Where are you?" "I'm here with you, Halo. Let's you and I go see the Heavenly Father now." "Oh, Master, that's wonderful! I've waited so long to see the Father." "I'm going there with you, Halo," Master said. "I'll see you there shortly."

"Master! I'm flying like the birds do. This is so exciting."

"Is that you, Master? I can see you now. Oh! There's Big Friend and Earth Father with him. I'm so glad to see my friends again. Master, I've never seen a more beautiful place than this, and I can feel the Father all through me. It's all just like you said it would be." "Yes, Halo, it is as I said it would be, but now I must return to earth again for I have more work to do. I'll see you again in forty days, but you must stay here and wait for me."

"I will wait, Master, with Big Friend and Earth Father. We'll wait for you."

The End

7084054R0

Made in the USA
Charleston, SC
20 January 2011